To Benjamin, Emily, Rebekah, and Katherine—
may you always have the courage to look for your own best happily-ever-afters
—V.B.

To my mom and the childhood I wish she could have had
—S.P.

Balzer + Bray is an imprint of HarperCollins Publishers.

The Princess and the Frogs
Text copyright © 2016 by Veronica Bartles
Illustrations copyright © 2016 by Sara Palacios
All rights reserved. Manufactured in China.
No part of this book may be used or reproduced in any manner whatsoever without written permission
except in the case of brief quotations embodied in critical articles and reviews. For information address
HarperCollins Children's Books, a division of HarperCollins Publishers, 195 Broadway, New York, NY 10007.
www.harpercollinschildrens.com

Library of Congress Control Number: 2015018702
ISBN 978-0-06-236591-0 (trade bdg.)

The artist used watercolor, graphite, and digital media to create the digital illustrations for this book.
Typography by Aurora Parlagreco
16 17 18 19 20 SCP 10 9 8 7 6 5 4 3 2 1
❖
First Edition

The Princess and the Frogs

Written by Veronica Bartles

Illustrated by Sara Palacios

Balzer + Bray

An Imprint of HarperCollins*Publishers*

Princess Cassandra should have been the happiest princess in the world. She had hundreds of dresses, thousands of books, and servants to bring her anything she wanted. There was only one thing she didn't have. A best friend.

"I want a pet that matches my favorite green dress," she said.
"We'll swim and jump and play all day. And at night, he will
sit on my pillow and sing to me."

The Royal Pet Handler searched for the perfect pet.
But it wasn't easy.

The mouse was too squeaky.
The kitten refused to swim.
The hippo wouldn't jump.
And none of the animals were green.

"I need a pet that's just right," Cassandra said.

So the Royal Pet Handler searched mountains and valleys, rivers and streams, until he discovered a little green frog with bumpy brown spots for the princess to love.

"He's perfect!" Cassandra declared.

The princess and the frog raced through the castle, jumped rope in the courtyard, and sampled treats in the kitchen.

After dinner, Cassandra tucked her new best friend into bed.
"Good night, Froggy." She kissed his bumpy green head.

Whoosh!

The frog turned into a prince.

He bowed and kissed Cassandra's hand.
"Thank you, Princess. Let us be married at once!"

She laughed. "Princes aren't pets. I want a frog!"
And she sent him to work for the Royal Pastry Chef.

Once again, the Royal Pet Handler searched
forests and meadows, ponds and lakes,
until he discovered a shiny green frog with
soft, smooth skin for the princess to love.

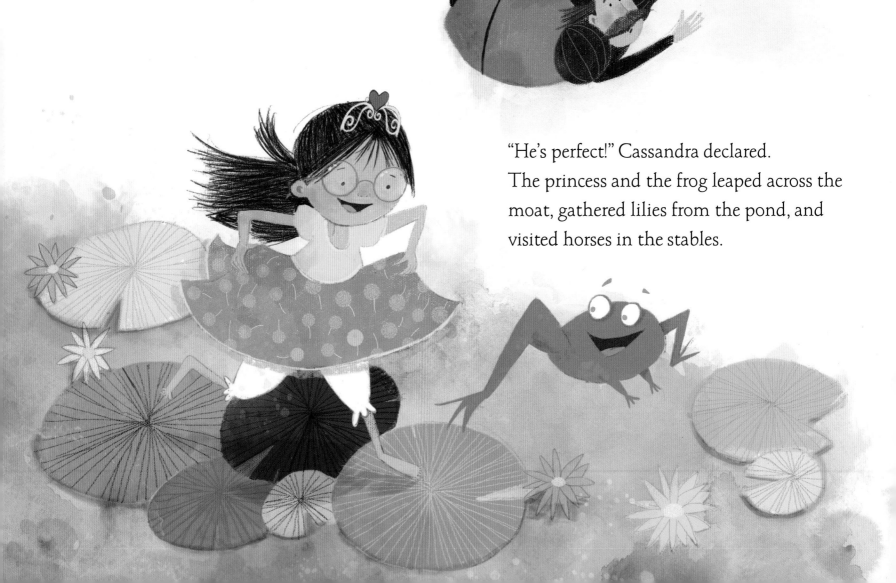

"He's perfect!" Cassandra declared.
The princess and the frog leaped across the
moat, gathered lilies from the pond, and
visited horses in the stables.

After dinner, Cassandra tucked her new
best friend into bed.
"Good night, Froggy." She kissed his
shiny green head.

Whoosh!

The frog turned into a prince.

He smoothed the wrinkles from his suit
and smiled at himself in the mirror.
"The spell is broken! We can be married
right away."

Cassandra frowned. "Princes aren't pets. I want a frog!" And she sent him to work for the Royal Stable Master.

Word of Cassandra's search spread, and one by one,
the people brought frogs to the palace.

FAT frogs.

small frogs.

BIG frogs.

But each turned into a prince when Cassandra kissed him good night. Soon she ran out of jobs for them.

"I don't need help," Cassandra said. "I'll find the perfect frog myself."

thin frogs.

She searched the pond, among lotus blossoms and lily pads, until she discovered a great green frog with a bright blue belly.

"He's perfect!" Cassandra declared. But the frog disappeared into the tall rushes on the bank.

"I love hide-and-seek!" The princess explored every cranny and nook until she found the frog in a clump of cattails. She scooped him up and carried him home.

After dinner, Cassandra tucked her new best friend into bed. But when she tried to kiss his head, he hopped away.

The great green frog with the bright blue belly was the best hide-and-seek player ever. Each time Cassandra found him, he hid again.

Finally, she caught him sleeping under her throne.
"There you are, Froggy!" She scooped him up into
a hug and kissed his great green head.

Whoosh!

"But I liked being a frog," the prince said.

"Princes aren't pets!" Cassandra cried.

But they were everywhere.

Sprawled across the royal beds.
Using her dresses as tails for their kites.
Smudging sticky fingerprints on the
best books in the library.

"I can have fun all by myself!" the princess declared.
So she sent the princes away.

Cassandra played in the empty courtyard
and read books in the silent library.

But even her favorite green dress didn't make her happy. And she still didn't have a friend.

Then one day, Cassandra discovered a bedraggled little prince
sniffling in the garden. "I have nowhere to go," he said.

Princess Cassandra sighed. "You can't stay here. Princes aren't pets."

"I don't want to be a prince." He sat on the steps and sobbed.
Cassandra wiped his tears with her handkerchief. "I'm sorry."
She kissed his curly head.

Spaloosh!

The prince turned into a great green frog with a bright blue belly.

Princess Cassandra scooped him up into a giant hug.
"I love you, Froggy."

And the princess and the frog lived happily ever after.

As long as she remembered *not* to kiss his great green head.